Welcome to Derry – The Cycle of Fear

Derry, Maine—a dot that flickers on maps yet burns bright in nightmares. From 1719 to 1954 the town wakes every twenty-seven years, heralded by bell-less chimes, masks that weld to skin, and rust-red balloons hovering on still air. Smell burnt sugar, hear a crooked waltz in the wind, and know the

buried heart of Derry is beating again—
waiting for you to come play.

Preface

by HeartBit

"Some stories echo like footfalls in an empty tunnel: you hear them once, and for the rest of your life you are never wholly sure whether the next step is yours or theirs."

I did not grow up in Derry, Maine—few of us did, because the town both is and is not on any map. Yet its pulse has throbbed in the background of my creative life like a distant fairground generator: an ever-present hum that powers equal parts terror, tenderness, and the giddy dare of saying *what if*.

This book, **Welcome to Derry – The Cycle of Fear**, is my attempt to walk the perimeter of that hum. It began as a private exercise in collage: photocopied headlines; fragments of Stephen King's lore; my own nightmares of green-burning campfires and sugar-scorched air. What you hold now is a spliced reel of those clippings, threaded with fresh narrative sinew and stitched into a timeline that spans more than two centuries. I have tried to keep the seams visible. If you see the glue—good. Horror should never let you forget the artifice even as it quickens your pulse.

A few points of orientation before we descend:

1. **Homage, not hijack.** These pages stand firmly on the shoulders of King's original creation. Every invented character, document, or calamity is a love-letter written in rust-colored ink. No canon has been displaced; only shadow-boxed.

2. **Anachronism is deliberate.** HeartBit is an "individual collective"—I write with multiple voices on a single set of vocal cords. Expect Victorian prose to glitch into nickel-odeon slang, then refract through a 1930s radio hiss. The monster underneath does not care about era-appropriate diction, so neither do I.

3. **Burnt sugar as leitmotif.** You will smell it often. Scholars debate whether the scent is psychic residue or chemical clue; I prefer to think it is childhood itself— half carnival, half crematorium.

4. **Cycle over climax.** Unlike a conventional novel, the book advances in pulses: 1719, 1742, 1769, and so on. Each pulse ends abruptly, like a match going out. If you find the blackout frustrating, take heart: that is how Derry's citizens live—lucid for a moment, then swallowed by the dark.

5. **The Mud Mice live.** Somewhere. Somewhen. If my telling feels unfinished, remember that unfinished things are harder to bury.

Why bother?

Because horror is a rehearsal for empathy. To imagine a cosmic predator that feeds on fear is to admit how much fear already feeds on us in real life—pandemic data streams, algorithmic dread, sirens at 3 a.m. Mapping Derry's disasters lets me confront the truth that every town, every family, carries its own periodic catastrophe. Horror simply turns the invisible inside-out and paints teeth on it.

If, while reading, you feel a child's giggle brush the back of your neck—good. Close the book for a moment. Listen harder. You may discover that the sound comes from nowhere. Or everywhere. Or from the page itself, bending just slightly in your grasp as if inhaling.

Either way, thank you for opening the cover and stepping into the clearing. If the ground feels warm, remember: that is only the story breathing beneath us.

Enjoy the ride—
and if the shadow roars again, meet me by the meteorite.
We'll bring matches we never strike.

— **HeartBit**
Dawn with fog on the Tiber, June 2025

BOOK I – *The Breathing Clearing* (1719 – 1728)

CHAPTER 1

The Imperfect Cartographer

[Field Diary — Jonas Hatch]

12 November 1719 – Reached a hollow north-east of the Kenduskeag. Air tepid as a dozing hound; grass exudes steam. Compass gyrates without pause. My horse refuses the brook—drinks instead from emptiness. Must observe.

The compass spun like a child's top, its needle kicking against the glass. Jonas Hatch steadied it, blinking through the low mist.

Hatch (muttering): "Magnetic iron? Lightning strike? Or merely the devil upending my declinations?"

The horse—an ageing bay named Sable— stamped and tossed her head.

Hatch: "Easy, girl. We'll camp, map, and be gone."

Sable: *snorts, ears flat*

By dusk he had pitched a small canvas lean-to. He struck flint to tinder. The tinder caught— but burned green, a sickly witch-light that painted the trees in jaundiced hues.

Hatch's eyes widened.

Hatch: "In Providence they'd call that *phosphor*. Here… well, best I keep the fire low."

He fed the flame sparingly. Greenness curled into the night like serpent smoke. Later, when embers should have died, they hissed—tiny serpents still alive and whispering. Hatch corked them in a tin.

Hatch (writing): *"Ashes collected. They breathe."*

He lay awake, listening to Sable's uneasy breathing—and to something beneath it, a slow subterranean pulse, as though the earth itself dreamt in its sleep.

CHAPTER 2

Crimson Roots

October came early the following year, dragging wet flurries behind it. Snowflakes reached the clearing, sizzling to nothing on contact. Hatch knelt, touch-testing the ground.

Hatch (to himself): "Cold air, warm soil. A hearth without fire."

He drew his knife, prying back a corner of moss. Oak roots, thick as an infant's arm, bled a scarlet sap. It oozed down the blade—viscous, half-resin, half-blood.

Hatch (softly): "Sap should amber in winter, not run like a butcher's spill."

Behind him came footsteps—Pierre Leclerc, a trapper hired as occasional guide.

Leclerc: "Mon ami, that tree is hurt—or cursed. Either way, leave it."
Hatch: "Cursed trees don't bleed… they weep pitch. This—"
Leclerc (crossing himself): "—is why I told the Penobscot I'd not linger after sundown."

They watched in grim silence as more trees bowed inward, their crowns leaning as though in reverence to something buried at their feet.

That night snow reached half a foot outside the clearing—inside, the ground remained bare, warm, and faintly thudding.

CHAPTER 3

The Map That Refused to Stay Drawn

Hatch stacked three weeks of surveys on the folding table. Every sunrise he traced boundary lines; every dawn the ink seemed to drift— contours eclipsed, landmarks skewed, all notes spiraling to a central knot.

He confronted his assistant, Benjamin Marks, a taciturn lad from Portsmouth.

Hatch: "Did you nudge my sheets?"
Marks (insulted): "Sir, I never touch your cartography."
Hatch: "Then the devil himself is the draughtsman."

He pinned the latest parchment with brass tacks, muttering a prayer.

Marks (after a long pause): "Sir... Could the land be... moving?"
Hatch (laughs, frail): "Land moves by inch— tectonics, frost-heave, erosion over decades. Not in the span of supper till sunrise."

Yet he stared at the spiraling lines and felt a nauseous certainty: the clearing *turned*, slowly, like a mouth deciding when to yawn.

That evening he inked one terse sentence in the margin: *"The ground moves when we aren't looking."*

Outside, wind combed dead leaves into a vortex mirroring the one on his map.

CHAPTER 4

Songs at Dawn

Seeking counsel beyond western science, Hatch rode south to a Penobscot camp. Morning fog swaddled bark-lodges; smoke curled from cedar fires. The elders received him in silence until the shaman, Kchi-Skotay, emerged—a stooped figure with eyes bright as obsidian.

Kchi-Skotay (in measured English): "You come from the place where earth breathes."
Hatch (cautious): "I study it, yes. The clearing north of the Kenduskeag. Something—unnatural—resides."
Kchi-Skotay: "Not unnatural. *Older.*"

The shaman produced a rattle carved from birch and painted with red spirals. It chimed like dried rain when shaken.

Kchi-Skotay: "Sky-womb fell, long before Penobscot stories. There, dreams eat light. Do not greet their song, cartographer."
Hatch: "Would knowledge not arm me?"
Kchi-Skotay (soft resonance): "Knowledge feeds it. Curiosity is meat."

He pressed the rattle into Hatch's hands.

Kchi-Skotay: "Carry this. If it trembles, do not answer. Turn away."

Hatch bowed, uncertain whether gratitude or dread weighed heavier.

That night, back at the clearing, frost silvered the grass, though the soil remained warm. In the dark hours before dawn, children's laughter drifted among the oaks—high, bright, impossible.

The rattle in Hatch's fist twitched on its own, beads clicking. He clenched harder.

Disembodied Voice (sing-song whisper): "Jonas… draw us closer…"
Hatch (hoarse): "No."

The laugh peeled again, closer, then tapered into a breath like wind sucked into a hollow trunk. The rattle stilled. Silence returned—save for the dull heartbeat beneath the earth.

Hatch added a final diary line at sunrise, ink trembling:

"I did not answer its song—but it heard mine all the same."

And somewhere underfoot, something enormous shifted, sighing back to sleep, content that the game had merely begun.

BOOK II – *The Week of Balloons* (1741 – 1742)

CHAPTER 1

Derry Is Born Twice

A detachment of red-coated settlers pitched palisades along the Kenduskeag in April 1741. They named the post **Fort Derry** after lieutenant-colonel Patrick Derry, who kept a Bible in one pocket and a flintlock in the other.

Grace Carroway—journeywoman metalsmith, copper curls pinned under a soot-streaked kerchief—hammered nail-plates for the storehouse while her eight-year-old daughter Daisy wandered the spruce fringe.

A thin melody drifted from the trees: high, lilting, almost playful. Daisy hummed it back.

Daisy (softly): "La-la-la… come follow me…"
Invisible Chorus (from the woods, in perfect imitation): "La-la-la… come follow *me*…"

Daisy froze. The echo multiplied, same pitch, same child-voice, a dozen mirrors of her own. She stepped toward the darkness between trunks.

Grace's hammer halted mid-swing.

Grace (calling): "Daisy Carroway, keep to the clearing!"
Daisy (startled): "Mama, the woods are singing my tune."
Grace (eyes narrowing): "Then hush it. Some songs aren't ours to answer."

That night Daisy recited the lullaby while Grace tucked her beneath a patchwork quilt. Each verse repeated from the treeline, fainter, fainter—until the final note whispered inside the cabin itself, directly behind Grace's ear.

CHAPTER 2

The Bell Without a Belfry

Mid-June, diggers struck metal beneath the parade ground. They hauled up a bell—three feet across, unmarked, bronze swirled with veins of greenish alloy that pulsed like fish scales.

Grace examined a sliver chiseled from the rim.

Grace (to Lt. Derry): "No foundry stamp, no maker's cut. Bronze shouldn't carry malachite so deep. Where in God's name did this form?"
Lt. Derry (shrugging): "Melt it down. Fort needs nails more than riddles."

The bell went to the forge. When it hit the crucible, the air filled with the smell of caramelized sugar—pleasant for a heartbeat, then acrid, throat-scorching. Violet steam rose in serpentine columns, searing any exposed flesh. Three smiths staggered out, blistered and half-blind.

The molten metal sang—a resonant hum like a choir locked in a barrel. Even after being cast

into nail-pigs, the iron-framed crates trembled
at odd hours, ringing with that same, low hymn.

CHAPTER 3

Autumn Balloons

By October 1742 the fort had grown into a settlement of forty-two buildings. Dawn of the sixth brought an impossible sight: rust-colored balloons—hundreds—drifting shoulder-high, perfectly still despite the breeze.

Children squealed; adults crossed themselves. The spheres were not leather nor paper—some waxy membrane warm to the touch. They bobbed above doorsteps, tethered to nothing.

Reverend Abel Kierce (voice quavering): "Heaven send signs, but hell sends parodies." **Field Surgeon Merriweather:** "If they're gasbags, a spark could—"

Pop. One balloon burst, releasing a shimmer of golden dust. Moths—clouds of them—billowed from the rooftops, drawn to the glitter like iron to lodestone. Each moth's wings bore swirling red dots, miniature spirals.

The popping continued through the night, a slow artillery: *pop-pop-pop,* dust dazzling beneath lantern-light, moths rattling against shutters like hail.

CHAPTER 4

The Landward Shipwreck

Heavy rain battered Derry on 8 October. The unfinished pier sheared from its pilings and slammed downstream; livestock floated belly-up alongside casks of barley.

At sunrise young Eben Willis found something lodged among reeds—a toy frigate, twelve inches long, paint unweathered. Tiny gilt letters on the stern read **S. S. PILGRIM**.

Nine children gathered to marvel; nine sets of shoeprints led away into the sodden road… and ended abruptly at a single round depression six feet wide, as though some giant foot had pressed the mud smooth.

Grace arrived minutes later, face ashen.

Grace (softly to Lt. Derry): "My Daisy is among the nine."
Lt. Derry (clenching jaw): "Search parties—lanterns, dogs—now."

They searched through sleet until dusk, finding only the frigate, rocking in a puddle that reflected no sky—only darkness spiraling inward.

CHAPTER 5

Star-Fire

All-Hallows' Eve, 1742. Clouds congealed in unnatural tiers—like petals of a night-blooming flower. At midnight the sky ignited: curtains of emerald, crimson, and bruised purple cascaded downward, *upside-down aurora* that licked rooftops with silent flame.

Buildings did not char; they sagged, softened, as though heat had melted their bones but spared the skin. Timber curled like wax under a lantern. Iron nails—those cast from the bell—throbbed, glowing sugary pink.

Five charred-but-living souls crawled from the wreckage at dawn. Each babbled the same vision to Reverend Kierce:

Survivor #1 (eyes glazed): "A mouth in the sky… smiled wider than the river…"
Survivor #2 (weeping): "…teeth like steeples… it *opened* and the light poured in…"
Reverend Kierce (stooping, terrified whisper): "You saw Judgment?"

Survivor #3 (laughs, a child's giggle in an adult throat): "Not judgment. Supper."

The settlement's records would later blame "chemical wildfire." But every witness remembered the same after-taste in the air: burnt sugar… and distant, delighted laughter echoing down from a sky that suddenly seemed much, much too close.

BOOK III – *Cycles of Blood*
(1769 – 1850)

Four tableaux, each 27 years apart, traced like bloody thumbprints on the ledger of Derry. New streets rise, surnames change, industries bloom—yet the same pulse ticks beneath the cobbles, counting time in dread.

1769 – *The Feast of Crows*

Fort-turned-village has become a modest river town. Then smallpox arrives by barge; coffins stack like cordwood. By mid-summer a cloud of crows blackens the sky, settling each dusk on the steeple of First Derry Church.

Twilight of the Ninety-Nine

Reverend Elias Cudmore steps onto the belfry balcony, lantern fizzing in the gloom. One hundred and one throats croak in ragged harmony—yet he counts only a hundred beaks.

Cudmore (hoarse prayer): "Lord, deliver us from carrion and contagion."
Verger Martha Pike (shivering): "I count ninety-nine, sir."

Cudmore (blanching): "No—there are more voices than wings."

A wind gust scatters feathers. One crow remains, larger, perched on the bell rope. Its eye glints a deep, ember red.

Crow (impossibly articulate, a child's lilt): "One hundred… and one."

The rope jerks; the bell tolls by itself. Doors slam across town; shutters rattle. Next morning every crow lies gutted on the green—except the largest, which is nowhere to be found. Scavengers find numbered pebbles in each carcass: *1 to 100*. The pebble *101* is missing.

1796 – *The Cinder Masquerade*

Prosperity returns: the new foundry throws a harvest ball. Guests swirl in felt masks and silken gloves beneath candelabra smoke.

Midnight Weld

Blind pianist **Enoch Byrne** glides fingers across the keys. He was hired for jigs, yet an eerie waltz unfurls—a tune no one rehearsed.

Byrne (quietly, to the piano): "Whose melody are you, little ghost?"

Dancers slow; couples lock step. At the sixth refrain felt stiffens, liquefies, seeps into skin. Masks fuse—flesh sealing like hot wax. Gasps muffled, laughs strangled.

Mrs. Adelaide Foye (clawing her cheeks): "My face—Lord, it burns!"
Dr. Maslin (mask half-melded): "Keep calm! Remove—" *skin tears* "—oh heavens!"

Byrne, unseeing, continues to play, sweat slicking ivory. A child's laughter swirls in the orchestra loft though no child stands there.

Lanterns gutter at 3 a.m. Dawn reveals twelve dancers collapsed in a ring: featureless ovals where faces had been, mouths erased. Byrne sits frozen at the piano—maskless, eyes blind but weeping bright red tears of candle wax.

1823 – *Doll-Road*

Derry boasts cobbled lanes and a lace mill. One September sunrise, cloth dolls appear on every doorstep—homemade, button-eyed, each chest stitched with a child's Christian name.

The Scissors Test

Seamstress **Hester Quinn** lifts a doll labelled *ALICE*—her own six-year-old's name. The doll is oddly heavy.

Hester (to her sister Nan): "Feel this. Stuffed with pebbles?"
Nan (frowning): "Smells like… burnt sugar."

Town rumor flies: dolls are devil talismans. That night a frightened father hurls his son's doll into the hearth. *Whoomf!*—green flare, then ash.

Two streets away the boy vanishes from bed without a rumple in the sheets. Footprints lead to the window, stop abruptly on the sill.

Councilman Pratt calls an emergency meeting. He slams a charred dolly on the table—it clunks like cast iron.

Pratt (voice cracking): "Thirteen children gone. These things weigh like gravestones!"

Old Mrs. Pike (from shadows): "They're full now—heavy with what they've taken."

Overnight, terrified parents stash the remaining dolls in the church crypt under lock and key. By dawn the crypt is empty—only tiny bow-shapes etched into the stone, as though hundreds of mouths had kissed the floor goodbye.

1850 – *The Hematite Mine*

Rail tracks snake into Derry's hills; miners drive shafts deep under the Barrens. On 12 May a blast reveals a cavern of living garnet, veins throbbing like arteries.

Red Water Rising

Foreman **Caleb Wickower** lowers a lantern; crimson facets pulse to its glow. He lays a gloved hand on a crystal column.

Wickower (awed): "Feels warm—heartbeat warm."
Miner Hodge: "Rocks don't beat, Caleb."
Crystal (deep thrum, felt not heard): THUMP—THUMP.

Water breaks through—black, oily, shimmering violet. Tunnels flood; men scramble up iron ladders, coughing metallic steam.

They surface near dusk. The whistle of the shift mill should buzz across town—silence instead. Streets stand deserted save for townsfolk, eyes shut, swaying gently, whispering in chorus.

Town Chorus (soft, tuneless): "La… la… la… la…"

It is the same lullaby Daisy Carroway once hummed over a century before.

Wickower shakes his wife's shoulders—she sways but will not wake. Across Derry every sleeper mouthes the wordless tune. In cellar light the miners watch lamp-flame pulse to their heartbeat; the water dripping off their boots gleams like liquid hematite.

As stars rise, the chanting stops. Sleepers blink, confused. No one recalls the song—but fifty-seven miners lie drowned below, lungs packed with black water that weighs as heavy as stone dolls.

By 1851 Derry's ledger lists these calamities as "acts of God, pestilence, and industrial misfortune." But a marginal note penned in tremulous hand repeats every 27 lines: "We feast, we dance, we play, we drown."

BOOK IV – *The Roaring Shadows* (1877 – 1904)

The railroad whistles, the factories boom, the gas-lamps flicker—and yet every ledger line in Derry is underscored by the same low chuckle. Below, three "primary sources" survive in courthouse archives, their margins brittle with soot and river-mold. Where the paper frays, the darkness fills in the words.

1. *Derry News* – Extra Evening Edition, 3 September 1877

(microfilm transcript)

GREEN LIGHTS STALK THE BARRENS – TWELVE BOYS VANISH

By *H. Colson Whitby, Staff Correspondent*

Residents along the Kenduskeag reported a **"phosphorescent carnival"** flaring above the Barrens shortly after nine o'clock last night. Witnesses describe **emerald beams pirouetting** through the fog and **"animals made of bottle-glass"** capering in silence.

Tommy Lachance, age 11: "They had lions you could see through, Mister—bones all crinkly. One roared like a jug o' wind."
Sheriff Harold Irons: "Summer hysteria, nothing more. Boys stay out after dark, start telling tales."

Lantern parties searched till dawn. At press time **twelve youngsters are missing**, last seen racing toward the riverbed. A single clue recovered: **footprints in creek-silt that end abruptly at a ring of scorched grass—no sign of flood or fire.**

Town elders urge calm. The *Derry News*, however, reminds readers of the **Crow Plague of 1769** and the **Cinder Affair of 1796**. History, it seems, repeats to the beat of an unseen drum.

[Editor's note: Type slugs for three paragraphs melted in the press; molten lead dripped into a grin-shape before hardening.]

2. *Scarborough Iron & Brass Co.* – Incident Report, 14 July 1896

(carbon copy, Foundry Archives Box 42; annotations in grease pencil)

Section A – Accident Summary

- **Event time:** 22:37, Night Shift

- **Kiln:** Cupola #3

- **Incident:** Molten iron exited taphole at 2780 °F; instead of forming ingots, the pour **"bulged upward into hemispheres"** which then **solidified into human-sized** *smiles.* Creases, dimples, even "implied laughter lines" present.

Section B – Eyewitness Depositions

Foreman Silas Greevey: "I swear the slag looked back at me—mouth wide as a furnace door."
Pattern-maker Elsie Penwright: "There was music in the ladle. A tink-tink like a toy piano."

Section C – After-Action Notes

1. *Product Diversion*: Thirteen "smiling casts" were cooled and—contrary to safety

protocol—sold off by junior clerk Crombie to antique dealers in Bangor.

2. *Secondary Loss*: Within seven days each item **disappeared from storefront displays**; shards of green glass found in their place.

3. *Olfactory Residue*: Entire bay still reeks of **burnt sugar and ozone.** Ventilation ineffective.

Superintendent's Signature: *[line broken, ink dribbled into the shape of a crescent grin]*

3. *Town-Council Minutes – Emergency Session*, 2 April 1904

(stenographer's shorthand later typewritten; marginalia by Recorder Phineas Lott)

09:03 a.m. – Chair gavel.
Roll: Mayor Ezra Chute, Aldermen Pike, Corcoran, Ellis, Webb; Town Engineer **Rune McTavish**; Clerk Lott.

McTavish (opening statement):

"Gentlemen, the new sewer-and-water grid hollows straight through shale once deemed impenetrable. Workers report *echoes*—a noise like an infant keening. When they sing to drown it, the pipes sing back."

Mayor Chute (laughs; minutes note 'nervous'):

"We're christening the mains at month's end. Derry must join the twentieth century, ghost stories be damned."

Motion: Approve Line-4 valve welds and schedule grand opening **for 30 April**. **Outcome:** Passed 5-0.

Marginal note by Clerk Lott: "Mayor joked the baby-cry might be 'the town being born again.' Entire chamber chuckled—except McTavish, who kept counting under his breath… to twenty-seven."

Post-Opening Addendum – *Police Docket, 30 April 1904*

- **10:00 a.m.** — Ribbon cut at Waterworks. Initial gush from hydrants **runs bright scarlet**, viscosity higher than expected. Crowd assumes prank with dye.

- **10:11 a.m.** — Engineer McTavish tests sample: liquid clots on gauze "**like arterial blood.**"

- **10:30 a.m.** — Mayor Chute excused himself, "queasy."

- **10:47 a.m.** — Body discovered in valve-house rafters. Chute hanged by fire-hose. Hose twists into a *smile* before sagging.

- **11:00 a.m.** — Water clears; no dye traced. Coroner lists cause of death "suicide under mental strain." Coroner's signature ends abruptly—the pen dented paper, ink pooled into small spirals.

These entries mark the final civic attempt to rationalize Derry's phenomena. By 1905 the phrase "Roaring Shadows" had slipped into local slang, used whenever streetlamps hummed or steam whistles wailed downriver—sounds that, to sensitive ears, always resembled distant, jubilant laughter.

BOOK V – *A Thousand October Eyes* (1931)

The Mud Mice—six kids who skip stones, swap ghost stories, and think they own every alley of Derry—learn by inches that the town owns them instead. What follows are ten brisk chapters, pinned to the calendar like rust-colored balloons.

1 *The Missing-Face Album*

Cast: Phoebe Quinn (13), eldest of the Mud Mice; Sam Corcoran (12), his pockets full of marbles; twins Teddy & Tom Lachance (11).

Phoebe wins a box Brownie at the Harvest Fair. She burns through a whole roll on the midway. When she develops the negatives, a tall blur rides the background—three meters off, then two, then one, edging closer frame-by-frame though Phoebe never recalls seeing him.

Phoebe (shoving prints under Sam's nose): "Six shots, six steps. Like he's playing Grandma's Footsteps with the shutter."
Sam (joking, uneasy): "Maybe you hired a

ghost for depth of field."
Phoebe: "Then why has he no face?"

The final photo shows only the blur's hand, sprayed across the lens from the inside.

2 *Kenduskeag's Roar*

Mid-month, Derry's upper dam ruptures during a cloudless night. The river bellows like a freight train. Mud Mice sprint to the embankment; mist hangs caramel-sweet.

Teddy (gagging): "Smells like burnt candy."
Nathaniel "Nate" Pike (10, runt of the gang): "My ma says sugar burns black before it turns gold."
Tom: "Shut up, professor."

They watch water—dark, viscous—gulp down trout and wheelbarrows alike. On the far bank something white bobs past: the papier-mâché clown from the fair, now eyeless.

3 *Hollow-Birch House*

Abandoned since quarantine days, the mill overseer's mansion moans in every wind. A gramophone needle scratches a record no one wound, spinning a waltz Phoebe later recognizes from an 18th-century newspaper clipping: "The Cinder Masquerade."

Jo "Firefly" Delgado (12, matches always in her boot): "No electricity, no phonograph key. Whoever's dancing, they cut in before us."

Floorboards breathe, wallpaper puckers like skin near flame. The record closes with a child's giggle that keeps spinning long after the music stops.

4 *Nathaniel's Dream*

Nate sleeps beneath the new stadium. He dreams twin moons blink open under the bleachers—pupils dilating until they swallow him whole. He wakes mid-scream, face pressed to red clay that pulses like a heart.

Next afternoon he sketches the eyes in charcoal; the circles fill the page, crowding one another, a thousand October eyes.

5 *The Candleless Vigil*

The gang decides on a night watch in the Barrens. Phantom glo-worms pepper the reeds. Sam strikes a match; a wind snuffs it. Ten matches later—*fssst... fssst...*—all go dark the instant flame licks sulfur.

Sam (voice cracking): "Wind's blowing wrong direction."
Phoebe: "No wind at all, Sam. Something's stealing the light."

They hear someone strike a match behind them; a sulfur flare outlines a grin too wide for any face. Then darkness again, deeper than before.

6 *Return of the Pilgrim*

Rain drains from the Barrens overnight, leaving a ditch dry as bone. Nestled there: the toy frigate **S. S. Pilgrim**, its deck sticky with fresh blood that soaks the wood yet never drips.

Jo (poking hull with a stick): "Ships don't bleed."
Nate: "Maybe this one does."

The stern nameplate peels like wet skin; underneath, new lettering scorches into place: **COME PLAY**.

Teddy vanishes two evenings later, last seen carving a mast from driftwood.

7 *Tunnel 27*

Searching for Teddy, the Mud Mice squeeze through a service hatch labelled "27." The storm drain slopes into a vaulted chamber veined with hematite, crystals glimmering red-black.

Phoebe (whispers): "A theatre."
Sam: "No audience, no exits."

A thrumming rises—*THUMP-THUMP*—matching heartbeats. Nate shields his eyes; in the facets he sees the missing boys dancing waltzes without feet touching ground. The gang flees, splashing through water that stains their shoelaces crimson.

8 *Frog Chorus*

Autumn frogs clog the riverbanks. Instead of croaks they chant names—soft, rhythmic recitations: **"Alice... Tobias... Daisy..."** the children lost in 1823, then 1742, then 1769.

Phoebe (shudders): "Even the frogs keep roll call."

Jo hurls a rock; the frogs fall silent, but the rock bounces as though the mud were rubber, leaving round prints like oversized toes.

9 *The Laughing Lamp-post*

Gas-lamps flicker orange on Halloween Eve. One bulb swells, glass warping into a jack-o'- lantern leer. Another follows, laughing in pops of escaping gas. Streets glow with hellish grins.

Sam backs away, slips, and the pavement opens like a mouth, swallowing him waist-deep before Phoebe yanks him free. His pant-legs bear teeth-shaped rips; sugar-burnt smell rises from the cloth.

Only five Mud Mice remain.

10 *The Seal Pact*

They gather by meteorite shard in Barrens clearing, knees muddy, hearts hammering.

Phoebe (voice steady): "If one of us calls, the others come back—no matter where, no matter when."
Jo: "And if *it* calls first?"
Nate (carving initials): "Then we answer louder."

They gouge initials: **PQ, SC, JD, NP**. Four marks. Teddy's and Tom's spaces bleed crystal dust that sizzles on the stone.

A wind rises, carrying distant calliope notes, or maybe just the river. The kids do not look back as they scatter home—four silhouettes under lampposts still chuckling.

EPILOGUE

The Night-Consumption Ledger

1 Municipal Health Board Extract – *12 November 1931*

Chairwoman Dr. Abigail Mallory, M.D.

"Forty-two deceased in twenty-three nights. All ages, no clear contagion vector. Lungs mottled, tissue necrotic only after dusk. We will log as *acute nocturnal phthisis*, likely fungal."

Alderman Webb (whisper): "Better mold than madness."

The motion passes; records are sealed. In the margin, Mallory's fountain pen dribbles a question she never speaks aloud: *Why do the corpses smell of burnt sugar?*

2 Coroner's Supplemental Autopsy Note

Case #27 — Corcoran, Thomas (age 11, twin).
— Lung tissue heavy, **dark crimson crystals** forming honeycomb structures.

– Pupils still dilated seventy-two hours post-mortem.

– Trace amounts of **caramelized sucrose** in bronchi.

Observation: Chest cavity resonated faintly during examination. Soundwave analysis inconclusive.

Signed—then hastily scratched out—by **Dr. Mallory**.

3 *Derry Sentinel* Editorial – 15 November 1931

MOLD OR MALEVOLENCE?
The Sentinel demands transparency. How does a healthy town lose forty-two citizens to "night air"? Rumors speak of river vapors, carnival chemicals, even *phantom lights*. Sheriff Daltry assures us the "Mud Mice" pranksters were not involved—though two of their number are among the dead.

We urge calm, curfews, and prayer. Above all, remember: **Derry endures.**

Typesetter's footnote: "Lead slug jammed; headline grin-shaped."

4 Journal of Reverend Silas Brann – 18 November 1931

"Buried nine children today. Coffins light as balsa; felt as though something already ate the weight out of them. When hymn ended, I heard a giggle. No one else near the grave."

Brann burns the entry, yet ash remains legible the next dawn.

5 Phoebe Quinn's Pocket Notebook – 1 December 1931

(Found decades later in a safety-deposit box)

"Rule of Four"

1. Never photograph shadows.

2. Never strike a match if you hear someone else do it first.

3. Never sail toy boats—rivers have teeth.

4. If one of us calls, **drop everything and run to Derry.**

Sam says we're lucky. Jo says luck tastes like iron. Nate just draws eyes. I pretend the camera's broken—but I keep fresh film. Something tells me we'll need proof, someday.

A smear of hematite dust coats the final page.

6 Unsent Letter – Sam Corcoran to Jo "Firefly" Delgado – 4 July 1945

Firefly,

Dreamt of lampposts laughing again last night. Woke to the smell of caramel and river-mud here in France, of all places. Thought it was trench smoke, but the Sergeant smelled nothing.

Do you *feel* Derry tugging? Nate wrote he's hearing music through steam vents at the Bangor railyard.

If the shadow roars—remember the initials on the meteorite. Meet there. No matches. Bring Phoebe's camera.

–Sam

The envelope is sprinkled with tiny green-glass shards that slice the paper from inside.

7 "Census Corrections" – Town Hall Ledger, updated 1954 (hand of Clerk Ruth Denbrough)

Columns revised quietly:

- **Cause of Death (1931):** *"Night-consumption outbreak"* → *"Data lost to flood damage."*

- **Children's Burial Lots:** Plot numbers scratched out; replaced with a single looping symbol → ☾

Ruth pauses, sensing eyes at the keyhole. Quill trembles: blot forms a perfect spiral.

Closing Whisper

Only four Mud Mice walked out of that October, their throats raw with secrets. For years they dispersed—war fronts, factory towns, camera desks—yet every sleep carried burnt-sugar wind and the faintest waltz.

They told no one. *Because telling feeds it.*

But diaries yellow, pipes groan, and something beneath Derry counts to twenty-seven.

When the tally ends—
the shadow will roar again,
and the Mud Mice will have to answer.

Postface

by HeartBit

"We survive the tale, or the tale survives us. Rarely both."

The last page has fallen shut; the rust-colored balloons have drifted beyond your peripheral vision—for now. If you have reached this point unscathed, congratulate yourself: you have walked Derry's centuries the way one crosses a frozen river—mindful that cracks form under every footstep, singing their thin, treacherous aria.

What remains?

A few embers:

- the hiss of green fire curling in your memory like an after-image;

- the faint taste of burnt sugar ghosting the tongue;

- the certainty that a child's lullaby can outlive its singer by lifetimes.

I keep these embers, too. While writing, I often paused at midnight, half-expecting the meteorite shard to pulse on my desk, or the pipes in my Roman apartment to echo with an infant's cry. Art imitates terror, yes—but terror is an excellent imitator in return.

Loose threads (intentionally untied)

1. **The missing Pebble #101.** You noticed its absence; so did I. Some voids should not be filled—only circled warily, like wells with no bottom.

2. **The red crystals beneath Tunnel 27.** A geologist friend tells me hematite cannot pulse. I nod, smile, and change the subject.

3. **Phoebe's undeveloped roll of film.** In drafts, I showed the photographs. They were more frightening unseen—our imagination dots the eyes better than any grain of silver nitrate.

Feel free to weave your own endings. Horror, after all, is an open-source genre.

Gratitudes, and one apology

- **Stephen King**, for gifting us a playground where even the slide chains rattle with myth.

- **The unnamed towns that inspired Derry**, from Bangor's foggy porches to the sundown silences of remote mill villages.

- **You, reader-traveler**, who dared the spiral staircase of timelines with me. Your heartbeat kept the corridor lights on.

And the apology: if tonight you dream of red water or smiling lamp-posts, blame these pages—but remember you turned them willingly.

Final cautionary hum

Every twenty-seven years, the shadow stirs. That arithmetic is fiction, yes, but fear knows its own calendar. In whatever city you inhabit, keep an ear out for untuned waltzes, for balloons that hover without strings. If you smell caramel where there should be ash, leave the match unstruck.

Should the roar come—as roars do—find a friend, carve initials into something that fell from the stars, and answer louder.

Until then, close the book, breathe easily, and let the clearing sleep.

I'll be listening with you.

— HeartBit
Late night, lamp-post chuckling somewhere outside, June 2025

HeartBit Manifesto

Individual Collective in Music, Words, and Visions

I am one. I am many.

HeartBit is born from the fragmented beat of an identity that refuses to be whole, to stay still. Every sound I produce, every word I write, every image I draw is a shard of me, refracting and multiplying.

I am not a group, yet I am never alone.

I am an individual collective: a single body telling its story through many voices. A continuous dialogue between the self and its doubles.

My music breathes, falters, cracks.

My words are caresses and edges, poems turning into noise.

My images are visions from an unmastered subconscious.

I do not seek coherence.

I seek resonance.

I seek fertile collisions between sound and silence, text and rhythm, image and void.

HeartBit is the plural of a self that stubbornly refuses to be defined.

And perhaps, in this very multiplication, I rediscover my voice.

Made in the USA
Columbia, SC
19 November 2025